McSpot's Hidden Spots
A Puppyhood Secret

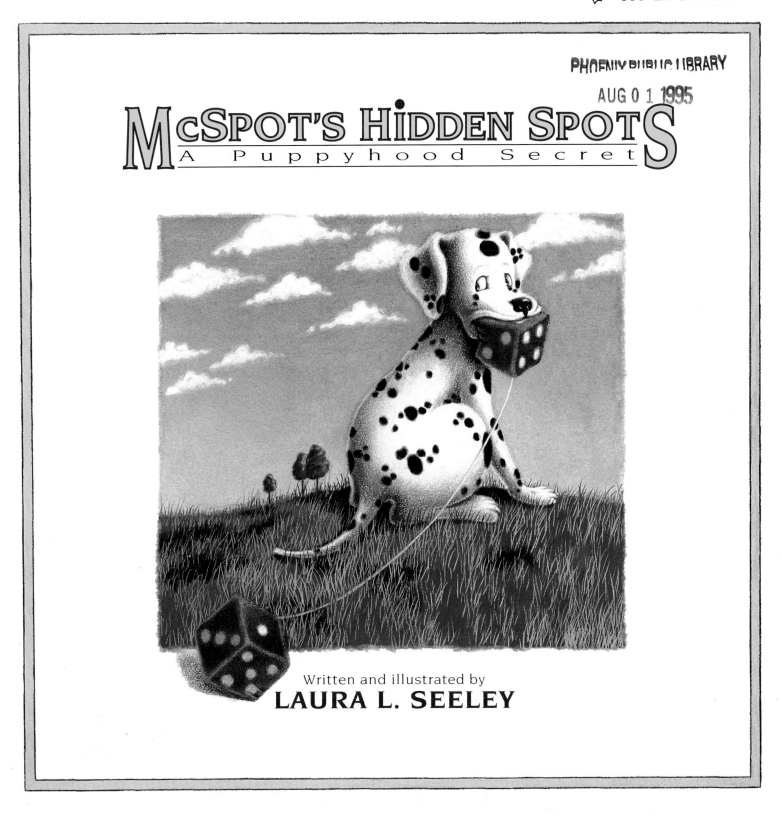

Written and illustrated by
LAURA L. SEELEY

PEACHTREE
ATLANTA

McSpot the Dalmatian, a spotted creation,
would boast that his spots made him best.
"I'm the number one creature because of this feature!
You all should be very impressed!"

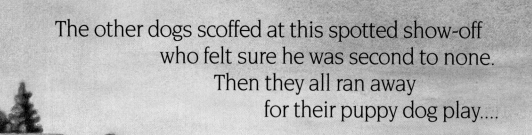

The other dogs scoffed at this spotted show-off
who felt sure he was second to none.
Then they all ran away
for their puppy dog play....

Around *him*,
they just didn't
have fun.

But the uppity pup
kept his nose pointed up,
quite convinced he was meant to be boss.
Those dogs were too crass,
and they didn't know class.
And besides,
it was clearly
their loss.

He grew terribly fond of a spot by the pond,
where he loved to observe his reflection.
With each look he just knew that it really was true—
he was painfully close to perfection.

Past the pond on the hill,
  his big secret and thrill,
was a spot in an old hollow tree.
Things with speckles and spots,
  even big polka dots,
  were brought here
  where nobody would see.

He had one thing in mind,
  to be king of his kind.
"I'm the spot king, I am!"
  thought the hound.
Other things that had spots
  tied his stomach in knots,
  so he stashed
  every spot
  that he found.

Then along came a day,
to his dappled dismay,
when McSpot found a shocking surprise.
What a sickening sight!
It was spotted and white!
And it watched him
with black, button
eyes.

"Another Dalmatian!"
he thought with frustration,
"Now *it* will get
all the attention!
"This simply can't be!
It looks too much like me!"
And he barked
at this spotted
invention.

It didn't bark back, and it wouldn't attack.
 It just stared with those black button eyes.
So he sniffed at its fur, but it still wouldn't stir,
 and McSpot felt his
blood pressure
rise.

On the spotted thing's head
was a ribbon bright red,
neatly tied in a beautiful bow.
Now he really was mad.
This was more than he had!
The new dog-thing with spots
had to go!

This was true spotted war,
and he dashed through the door
with a fearless and firm puppy grip,
taking care as he trotted that nobody spotted
his button-eyed dog-stealing trip.

He snuck past the pond to the tree just beyond
where he'd hidden that polka-dot pile.
"Such a dognapping job!"
thought the spotted pup snob,
and he tossed it
right in
with a smile.

He stretched and he sighed, feeling quite satisfied,
and decided to snooze for awhile.
He would stay the spot king,
and no spotted dog-thing
would be cramping
his slick puppy style.

What a frightening dream!
What a fur-raising scene
of him taking a bath
in a pail.

All that
bubbly fluff had been
spot-cleaning stuff
and had washed
off his spots,
head
to
tail!

What a nightmarish sight,
all that plain, puppy white!
And he ran to the pond,
very worried.
Feeling quite insecure,
he just had to be sure
that he still had his spots,
so he hurried!

Upon eager inspection,
he found his reflection.
His spots were still there!
And he sighed....
But his sigh of relief
was remarkably brief,
and his puppy dog eyes
opened wide.

First he spotted a duck and a wading woodchuck
that were covered with speckles and spots.
He saw more on a skunk and a chewing chipmunk,
and his stomach got tied up in knots.

"A polka-dot bird!
This is simply absurd!"
thought McSpot as he fought off the jitters.
"And four spotted fish!
This is just devilish!
Where on earth can I hide
all these critters?"

There were more on a moose
and a fox and a goose
and a bunch on the
back of a bear.
There were critters galore!
Spotted beasts by the score!
How unfair!
What a spotted
nightmare!

The spotted dognapper who'd once felt so dapper
looked down at his spots with a whine.
Now what would he do? All the rest had them, too,
and now spots didn't seem all that fine!

His puppy head ached. How much more could he take?
Was this still some ridiculous dream?
Was he getting paid back for his polka-dot stack
and his button-eyed dognapping scheme?

Then he hollered
a howl
as a huge, spotted owl
snatched him up,
and he thought he'd be swallowed.
While his puppy nerves jumped,
and his puppy heart thumped,
they flew off
to the tree
that was hollowed.

McSpot cried, "Not me!"
when he spotted the tree,
but the owl dropped him in with a "WHACK!"
At the owl he glared while the animals stared
at the pup on his
polka-dot stack.

"What a shameful display
to be treated this way!"
thought McSpot
as he sat with a scowl.
"I'm supposed to be great,
not
some spotted bird bait
for an impolite,
oversized
owl!"

What a bullying bird!
But then something
  occurred to McSpot,
  and he felt
  like a fool.
For he'd done
  the same thing
to become the spot king,
  acting sneaky
    and snobby
    and cruel.

He glanced under his chin
at his little stuffed twin,
and it seemed
to observe him,
unblinking.
It was timid and teeny.
He'd been such a meany.
How *could* he
have been
so
unthinking?

He felt bad underneath, a bit ugly beneath
all his spots about which he had chattered.
He'd seen only one thing,
        just that perfect spot king,
    but the "underneath" part
        was what
            mattered.

McSpot
felt like crying,
but spots started flying
around

and around

and around....

...then he tumbled and twirled
through a spot-flooded world
full of critters
and things
he had
found.

"I want to wake up!"
thought the polka-dot pup,
still asleep in his polka-dot dream.
The owl screeched "HOO!"
then he heard something "MOO!"
and McSpot
burst awake
with a scream.

He opened his eyes
as a face of great size
lowered
down
for a close-up inspection.
It had spots by the score,
like McSpot's,
but much more...

and it licked him
with spotted
affection.

In a world full of spots there would always be lots,
and McSpot finally figured this out.
Though he felt pretty small,
he was part of it all,
and he'd heard
that's what life
was about.

The stuff in the stack? Well, he took it all back;
it was no longer fun like before.
With more *heart* and less *pride* he felt better inside,
knowing no one can win a spot war.

He got used to his part in this spot-sharing art.
This was now the new pledge he was keeping
(though he still felt some knots, teeny-weenie sized knots
when he stared at a ladybug creeping).

And McSpot never knew something speckled and new
found that spot in the old, hollow tree,
just the place for providing and perfect for hiding

a secret or two...

even three.